# THE
# LION KING

$A$nimals came from far and wide to celebrate the birth of King Mufasa's son. When Rafiki, the wise, old mystic, stood at the edge of Pride Rock and held the infant high, all the animals bowed before Simba, their new prince.

Only Mufasa's brother, Scar, did not attend the ceremony. "Is anything wrong?" Mufasa asked him.

"It must have slipped my mind," lied Scar. But in fact, he was jealous. Simba had taken his place as next in line to be king.

When Simba was a little older, Mufasa led him one morning to the top of Pride Rock. "Everything the light touches is our kingdom," Mufasa said. He explained that one day, it would all belong to Simba.

"What about that shadowy place?" asked Simba, looking around.

"That is beyond our borders. You must never go there," Mufasa said.

But later that day, Simba's uncle Scar told him the place was an elephant graveyard. "Only the bravest lions go there," he said. Simba had no idea that Scar was setting a trap to get rid of him.

Simba wanted to prove he was brave, so he decided to visit the graveyard anyway. He invited his best friend, Nala, to go along.

"It's really creepy!" Nala said when they found a huge skull. But before the cubs could explore further, they were attacked by three hyenas. Luckily, Mufasa showed up in time to save them.

"Don't you ever come near my son again!" he roared.

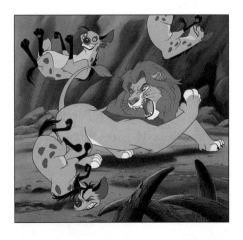

When they returned home, Simba explained, "I was just trying to be brave — like you, Dad."

"Being brave doesn't mean you look for trouble," Mufasa said.

That night, Mufasa showed Simba the evening sky. "The great kings of the past look down on us from those stars," Mufasa said. "They will always be there to guide you . . . and so will I."

But soon after, Scar lured the cub into another trap. This time, he arranged for Simba to be caught in a stampede of wildebeests.

Then Scar yelled to Mufasa, "Quick! Stampede! Simba's down there!"

Mufasa leaped into the gorge and snatched the cub out of the path of the deadly hooves. He set Simba safely on a rocky ledge, but then the rock crumbled under Mufasa's paws, and he fell.

Badly injured, he tried to crawl out again. He asked for Scar's help, but Scar pushed him into the stampeding herd.

Simba did not see Scar, but he saw his father fall. Simba raced into the gorge. But the great Lion King was dead.

Scar appeared out of the dust. "Simba," he said, "what have you done?"

"He tried to save me," Simba answered.

"If it weren't for you, your father would still be alive!" Scar told him. "Run away, Simba . . . run away and never return!"

Confused and heartbroken, Simba began to run. He did not see the hyenas join Scar, or hear his uncle order them to get rid of him once and for all.

The hyenas chased the cub to the edge of a plateau. There was only one way out. He leaped off the edge into a tangle of thorns. "If you ever come back, we'll kill you!" the hyenas shouted.

Injured and exhausted, Simba
stumbled across the hot African
desert. Vultures circled above him.
Finally he fainted. When he opened
his eyes again, a meerkat and a
warthog were standing over him.

"You okay, kid?" asked the meerkat.

"You nearly died," said the warthog.
"We saved you."

"Where ya from?" the meerkat asked.

"It doesn't matter," Simba said
quietly. Then he admitted, "I did
something terrible . . . but I don't
want to talk about it."

"Then you're an outcast!" cried the meerkat. "So are we! My name's Timon, and this is Pumbaa. Take my advice, kid. You gotta put your past behind you. No past, no future — no worries. *Hakuna matata!*"

So Simba followed Timon and Pumbaa to their jungle home. Time passed, and Simba grew into a young lion. He led a carefree life, although when he thought about his father, he grew sad.

One day, Simba heard his friends cry for help. He found Pumbaa caught beneath a fallen tree, while Timon tried to protect him from a hungry lioness. Simba pounced on her, and they tussled until the lioness recognized him. "Simba?" she said.

"Nala?" he replied.

"What's going on here?" asked Timon in confusion.

Simba introduced everyone, but Nala could not stop staring at him. "Everyone thinks you're dead," she said.

As they strolled through the jungle, Nala tried to convince Simba to return home and take his place as king. "Scar let the hyenas take over the Pride Lands," she said. "Everything's destroyed. If you don't do something soon, everyone will starve."

But Simba insisted he could not go back. They argued until Simba told Nala to leave him alone.

That night, Simba was still thinking about his decision when an old baboon appeared.

"I know your father," he said.

"My father is dead," Simba replied.

"Nope! He's alive. Just follow old Rafiki," the baboon said. He led Simba to a pool and pointed to Simba's reflection. "You see?" Rafiki said. "He lives in you!"

Then Mufasa's image appeared in the stars. "You must take your place in the Circle of Life," Mufasa said. "Remember who you are. You are my son and the one true king."

So Simba headed home to challenge his uncle. As he crossed into his kingdom, he saw devastation everywhere. The great herds were gone.

Meanwhile, Simba's mother was trying to convince Scar that they should leave Pride Rock in search of food.

"We're not going anywhere," Scar growled.

"You are sentencing us to death," Sarabi replied.

"Then so be it. I am the king and I make the rules!"

"If you were half the king Mufasa was...," Sarabi began. Enraged, Scar struck her.

As Sarabi fell, Scar heard a roar. He turned and saw a great lion. "This is my kingdom now," Simba proclaimed. "Step down, Scar."

But instead Scar gestured to the hyenas. "But they think I'm king," Scar said, and he backed Simba off the cliff. As Simba hung onto the edge by his claws, Scar sneered, "Where have I seen this before? Oh yes . . . that's just the way your father looked before I killed him."

Simba gathered all his strength and leapt toward his uncle. They fought viciously.

Meanwhile, Nala and the lionesses arrived with
Timon and Pumbaa to drive away the hyenas.
In the confusion, Scar tried to run away.

When Simba cornered him on Pride Rock, Scar
tried to talk his way out. "I didn't kill your
father. It was the hyenas. They are the enemy,"
he said.

Simba repeated the advice Scar had given him
years before. "Run away and never return,"
he commanded.

When Scar lunged at Simba again, Simba hurled him off the cliff. The sound of hungry hyenas drifted up from the gorge, revealing Scar's awful fate.

As rain began to fall, Simba stood at the edge of Pride Rock and roared triumphantly. The lionesses roared back with joy.

Soon, under the rule of the wise and brave Simba, the Pride Lands flourished. The herds returned to graze, and food was plentiful again. Not long afterwards, the animals gathered once more to celebrate the birth of the king's son.

Simba and Nala watched proudly as Rafiki held their new cub high over Pride Rock.

Simba remembered something his father had told him. "A king's time as ruler rises and falls like the sun. One day the sun will set on my time here and rise with you as the new king."

Someday Simba would pass on these same words to his son.